P9-CFZ-275

3 5674 02767384 8

JE

(Holiday)

APR 2 9 1998

Where's Prancer?

STORY AND PICTURES BY

SYD HOFF

 HarperCollinsPublishers

Copyright © 1960, 1988 by Syd Hoff · Printed in the USA.
All rights reserved. 1 2 3 4 5 6 7 8 9 10
❖ Newly Illustrated Edition
Library of Congress Catalog Card Number: 96-45028

It was early in the morning
when Santa Claus returned to the North Pole
after his big trip all over the world.

"I'm tired and I guess you are, too," he said to the reindeer. "So suppose you get to the stable and I'll see you all later."

Santa went into the house and had a nice hot cup of tea.

Then he put eight fresh carrots in a basket
and took them out to the stable.

"Here, Dasher, Dancer, Prancer, and Vixen,"
he said. "Here, Comet, Cupid, Donner, and
Blitzen—here's a nice carrot for each of you."

There was one carrot left over!

"One reindeer is missing," said Santa.
"Who is it?"

"It isn't I," said Dasher.

"It isn't I," said Dancer.

"It isn't I," said Vixen.

"It isn't us either," said Comet, Cupid, Donner, and Blitzen.

"It's Prancer," said Santa.
"Where can he be?"

"He was with us in Australia," said Dasher.
"He was with us in Sweden," said Dancer.
"He was with us in the Philippine Islands,"
said Vixen.

"He was also with us in Sioux City, Iowa,"
said Comet, Cupid, Donner, and Blitzen.

"Keep thinking, boys," said Santa. "If we don't get Prancer back, there may never be another Christmas. Everybody knows I have to have eight reindeer."

The telephone rang.

"Maybe it's Prancer!" cried Santa.

It was only a wrong number.

There was a knock on the door.
"Maybe it's Prancer!" cried Santa.

It was only a walrus knocking ice off his flippers.

"We remember," said the reindeer.
"It was Philadelphia. That was the last place
we saw him."
"Quick, to the sleigh!" shouted Santa.
"There isn't a second to lose!"

In the twinkling of an eye they were in
the City of Brotherly Love.
"Spread out now and look," said Santa.

Dasher went up Market Street, but all
he saw was a cat.

Dancer went up Broad Street, but all
he saw was a dog.

Vixen went into Fairmount Park, but all
he saw was a squirrel.

Comet and Cupid met at Independence Hall.

"A fine structure," said Comet.

"Yes," said Cupid, "but where's Prancer?"

"Here he is!" shouted Donner.

"That's only your reflection," said Blitzen.

A police car drove up. "A reindeer was just reported on Chestnut Street. Did you lose one?" asked the policeman.

"Yes," said Santa. "Thank you. We'll go get him."

Sure enough, there was Prancer.

"Where have you been?" said Santa.

"We were worried about you."

"I just wanted to see how people look on Christmas Day," said Prancer. "We always get here the night before."

"Let's all see," said Santa.

They saw many happy faces and were glad
they had helped make them that way.
Then Santa said, "Now we must go home."

Prancer sat with Santa and enjoyed the ride.

Once more Santa made himself a nice hot cup of tea and once more he took eight fresh carrots out to the stable.

This time there was none left.

Merry Christmas!